The
FLIGHT of
LEONARDO

Wyatt & Sons Publishers books may be ordered through booksellers or by contacting:

Wyatt & Sons Publishers, LLC
Mobile, Alabama 36695
www.wyattpublishing.com
editor@wyattpublishing.com

Because of the dynamic nature of the Internet, any web address or links contained in this book may have changed since publication and may no longer be valid.

Cover design by: Mark Wyatt
Interior design by: Mark Wyatt

ISBN 13:978-1-954798-33-5
Printed in the United States of America

The FLIGHT of LEONARDO

by
THOMAS PATRICK

WYATT & SONS
PUBLISHERS, LLC
Mobile, Alabama

DEDICATION

This book is dedicated to the young at heart
who dare to follow their dream.

PREFACE

Leonardo da Vinci was a man ahead of his time. A visionary whose mind spanned art, science, and engineering, he left behind a legacy that continues to intrigue and inspire. Best known for masterpieces like the Mona Lisa and The Last Supper, da Vinci was also an inventor, anatomist, and dreamer—one who constantly sought to unravel the mysteries of the world around him.

When Leonardo da Vinci was dying, he left all his works and sketches to his assistant, Francesco Melzi, who guarded them with his life. But after Melzi's death, Leonardo's writings fell into the hands of his pupil, Pompeo Leoni. Leoni, a sculptor, organized the drawings into albums and sold them to collectors. Many of da Vinci's writings were said to be lost—scattered across the world, hidden away in private collections, and some even rumored to have been sold on the illegal market.

But what if history did not capture all da Vinci's discoveries? What if hidden among his lost writings were ideas and experiments that had never been revealed, concepts far beyond what the world has ever known?

Leonardo da Vinci's obsession with flight led him to design several ornithopter-style flying machines, inspired by birds. While there is no verified record that he personally attempted flight, a legend from around 1505 suggests one of his apprentices launched one of Leonardo's flying devices from Monte Ceceri near Florence. The attempt reportedly ended in a crash that broke the apprentice's leg, prompting Leonardo to return his focus to painting and scientific study. Though likely apocryphal, the story reflects Leonardo's daring imagination.

Leonardo da Vinci was a firm believer that nature was the truest consultant for color and was obsessed with the properties of materials. In his quest to perfect the pigments used in his paintings, he experimented with finely ground minerals, metals, and organic substances, seeking colors that would not fade with time. Some accounts suggest that he may have even ground gold, silver and bronze into fine powders, blending them with clays and other elements in precise ratios to achieve a radiant, lasting pigment.

His search for the perfect color led him to experiment with many unusual materials, but what if, in doing so, he accidentally discovered something much more powerful than just a new pigment?

Centuries later, in the present day, a young man named Thomas Patrick is about to stumble upon something extraordinary. A dreamer at heart, Thomas has always been fascinated by the idea of flight, much like da Vinci before him. What he doesn't realize yet is that he is about to embark on a journey that will change everything—one that will take him from the pages of history to the edge of the impossible.

This story is about more than just an ancient secret lost in ancient writings, it is about the power of curiosity, danger in the pursuit of the impossible, and the fine line between legend and reality. Thomas would soon realize that some dreams never truly die – they simply wait for the right person to bring them to life.

This is the story of -- The Flight of Leonardo.

CHAPTER 1

A DREAMER IN THE MAKING

A lone bird glided past the classroom window at Saint Dominic's Catholic School, its wings stretched wide as it rode the air currents with ease. Thomas Patrick watched it with quiet fascination against the blue-sky background, tapping his pencil absently against the desk. He imagined what it would feel like to soar like that, to leave the world below and drift weightlessly through the air without boundaries.

"Thomas", a sharp voice cut through his daydream.

His head snapped forward. Sister Loretto, his teacher, stood at the front of the room, arms folded. The rest of the class had already turned to look at him.

"Would you like to share with the class what you find so fascinating outside the window?" she asked.

Heat rose to Thomas's face. He straightened in his chair, searching for words, but Sister Loretto didn't wait for an answer. She sighed and shook her head.

"Since you're so interested in what's happening outside my class, I want you to write a report on it and share it with the class first thing in the morning."

A few students snickered. Thomas groaned quietly but nodded. There was no point in arguing, but he was visualizing in his head and didn't think it was going to be a problem. The only problem he might have was how they were going to receive what he was going to share about the truth that was inside of him.

That evening at home, Thomas sat at his desk, flipping through the worn pages of his notebook. Sketches of wings and scribbled notes filled the margins. He picked up his pencil and began writing, his thoughts spilling onto the page.

"Since the beginning of time, man has looked to the skies and wondered what it would be like to fly. Birds glide effortlessly, their wings catching the wind, carrying them to places beyond our reach. Throughout history, brilliant minds have attempted to crack the code of human flight – none more than the great Leonardo da Vinci. He studied birds and bats, designed wings, and filled his notebooks with ideas centuries ahead of their time. What if he had succeeded? What if, long before the Wright brothers, Leonardo had built something that could truly take flight."

His hand moved quickly, tracing new lines, refining old ideas. He wrote about the bird he had seen, how effortlessly it moved through the air. He described da Vinci's sketches, the ornithopter, and his own ideas on what it would take to make a manual machine that could truly fly.

For the first time, he wasn't just dreaming about flight—he was putting it into words.

The next day, Sister Loretto motioned Thomas to the front of the class to read his paper first thing. Thomas walked up and stood at the front of the classroom, paper in hand. His desk was midway back of the room next to Izabella, a secret crush.

"Here goes" Thomas said quietly to himself. His voice was steady as he read his report aloud, the words flowing with more confidence than he expected.

The moment he started speaking, the classroom grew silent. As he described the dreams of mankind and the brilliance of Leonardo da Vinci, his passion took over. The words flowed effortlessly, painting a picture of soaring through the sky, defying gravity, and the endless possibilities that could come from unlocking the secrets of flight.

When he was finished, he lowered his paper. There was a pause. Then, the class erupted into applause. Sister Loretto, though she didn't smile, gave him a small nod of approval. Even Izabella was moved by his talk. It seemed she had a similar interest. Who knew?

As Thomas sat back down, his heart pounded with excitement. He had never felt so sure of anything before. This wasn't just a school assignment. This was a vision, a dream that had taken hold of him – a dream that one day, he would bring to life.

Sister Loretto walked over to the window and said, "Maybe there is something interesting outside that window after all."

Young Thomas never imagined that one day he would actually be proving the flight of Leonardo was possible.

Izabella listens to Thomas read his assigned report.

CHAPTER 2

THE MUSEUM ENCOUNTER

15 years later

Fall, 1986

Thomas Patrick stood in the quiet cemetery, surrounded by family and friends who had gathered to say their final goodbyes to his grandfather. The man who had instilled in him a deep sense of curiosity and a love for history was now gone. Thomas wished he had more time to spend with him, more time to learn from him. But even in death, his grandfather had left him something invaluable – his home - a place filled with artifacts, books, and mysteries waiting to be uncovered.

Thomas was a lot like his grandfather and much closer to him than the rest of the family. His grandfather had always encouraged him to follow his dreams, to never stop searching for answers. Now, as Thomas stood at the gravesite, he felt a renewed determination to live up to those expectations.

In the weeks after the funeral, Thomas took some time off work to settle into the house, going through his grandfather's belongings, reminiscing about the past. But one distraction kept calling to him – the new Leonardo da Vinci exhibit at the Mobile Museum of Art. The idea of seeing da Vinci's actual sketches and designs up close was irresistible and necessary. This small decision would change his life in amazing ways.

The next morning, taking a break from all the packing and sorting, Thomas drove the route to the museum. The familiar tree-lined streets brought back childhood memories of field trips and rainy afternoons spent wandering its halls. Today, however, was different. Today he wasn't just a visitor. He was a man searching for something – something he couldn't quite define yet.

Inside, the museum was bustling with guests but Thomas was drawn to the center exhibit, where a young employee of the museum was giving a tour. As he approached, her voice rang out clearly: "In this room, you will find a life-size functioning replica of the wings Leonardo da Vinci designed," she said as she gestured toward the impressive structure suspended from the ceiling. "Leonardo was fascinated with the concept of human flight and spent years studying birds, bats and air currents to develop his ideas."

Thomas froze. The voice. It was familiar. As he moved closer, he caught a glimpse of her face, and recognition struck him like a lightning bolt. It's Izabella!

She was standing before the group, confidently leading the tour, her dark eyes shining with enthusiasm. He hadn't seen her in years – not since their days at St. Dominic's School.

Before he could say a word, she turned slightly, her gaze scanning the crowd. Then, her eyes locked onto his.

A small, surprised smile played on her lips. "I remember you," she said, her voice carrying a hint of amusement. "As a matter of fact, you're part of my daily tour routine."

Thomas hesitated, then he said "I can't believe you recognize me."

"Of course I do," she said. "You're the one who gave that report on flying, back in the eighth grade." She apparently mentioned his story in every da Vinci tour, remembering a boy who dreamed of flying.

Thomas chuckled, scratching the back of his head. "I didn't realize I was so memorable."

Izabella's smile deepened. "How could I forget? It was one of the most passionate reports I'd ever heard. I Remember thinking – this guy is either a genius or completely crazy about flying."

Before Thomas could respond, she returned her attention back to leading the tour and continued speaking to the group.

"When Leonardo da Vinci was dying, he left all his works and sketches to his assistant, Francesco Melzi, who guarded them with his life. But after Melzi's death, Leonardo's writings fell into the hands of his pupil, Pompeo Leoni. Leoni, a sculptor, organized the drawings into albums and sold them to various collectors. Many of da Vinci's writings were said to be lost and no one knows what they contain... maybe even secrets."

As she spoke, Thomas noticed two men moving toward the front of the tour group, inching closer to Izabella. Something about them seemed off. They weren't admiring the artifacts like the rest of the visitors – they were focused on Izabella.

She saw them too.

Though she kept her composure, Thomas could see a flicker of unease in her eyes. These men weren't here for the exhibit. They were after something else.

Thinking quickly, Thomas stepped forward, closing the distance between himself and Izabella, creating a barrier between her and the men. They hesitated for a moment, exchanging glances, before subtly retreating toward the back of the group.

As the tour wrapped up, Thomas and Izabella walked together toward a quieter area of the museum.

"Who were those two strange men?" Thomas asked.

Izabella sighed. "I don't know, but they've been hanging around the museum a lot lately since the start of the exhibit. They're asking a lot of questions about Leonardo da Vinci's lost writings and drawings."

Thomas's heart pounded. "Lost writings?"

She nodded. "There are theories that some of da Vinci's notes and sketches were never recovered. Some believe they contained ideas and discoveries far ahead of his time. Some things that could even change everything we know about science and technology."

Thomas hesitated. Should he tell her? --like Clark Kent wanted to tell Lois Lane he was Superman.

Thomas possessed something that no one could ever imagine was now his – some of Leonardo's da Vinci's long lost papers hidden away in his grandfather's artifact room.

But before he could speak, Izabella continued. "Those men slipped out of the group and left the exhibit hall. I have no idea when they'll be back but I have a feeling they will."

Thomas felt a chill run down his spine. If those men knew about the lost papers, how far would they go to get them? And how long before they discovered he had them?

The world of discovery, danger, and romance was only just beginning...

Izabella leading the Leonardo da Vinci tour.

CHAPTER 3

THE ARTIFACT ROOM

Thomas invited Izabella over to his grandfather's house, saying he had something to share with her that could change the world. She agreed, curious about what had made him so bold and determined.

"Is he asking me out?," she thought. "Can't be. That's not world changing. Is it?"

The artifact room was rare for a home in Mobile, Alabama, but Thomas's grandfather had had one specially constructed for his work. It was sealed by a thick steel door, heavy and reinforced like something from a bank vault. Set half underground, it was reached by a narrow flight of steps that descended from the back of the house. The walls were lined with concrete, the air cool and still. Thomas's grandfather had built it to last—fortified against time, weather, and anyone who might come looking for what was inside.

Thomas led the way, unlocking the door and stepping carefully onto the lower floor, and turned on the small desk lamp his grandfather had rigged to a wall socket. Izabella followed him in, her eyes adjusting as she took in the tall shelves, covered tables, and trunks along the walls.

"Are you sure it's okay we're down here?," she asked softly, glancing at the shelves filled with books, bottles, and rolled parchments.

"He left the house to me." Thomas said. "I think this is why. He wanted me to find all this."

He crossed to a wooden chest near the far wall. Inside were notebooks and old papers bound with twine. He untied one bundle and spread the pages across the desk.

"What is all this?" Izabella whispered, stepping closer.

Thomas handed her a sheet. "Sketches. Some are exact copies of da Vinci's designs—but others... I haven't seen these in any books. I think they might be originals."

One page depicted a set of mechanical wings, detailed with pivoted joints, gears, and stretched fabric. They looked like something out of a dream—or a prophecy. Another page was filled with strange notes and formulas. Symbols for gold and silver were familiar, but others were harder to place.

Izabella tilted the paper. "Wait... this writing—it's backwards."

Thomas looked closer. "Mirror script."

"Leonardo used it all the time," she said. "Wrote from right to left. Some people think it was to keep his work private... others think it was just because he was left-handed."

She studied the page again. "This isn't English either. This is... Italian. Tuscan Italian. That's what he spoke."

Thomas reached into the chest and pulled out a worn leather journal—his grandfather's. He opened to a bookmarked page filled with translations, handwritten notes, and side-by-side mirror-script decodings.

"My grandfather figured out how to decipher them," he said. "He left a guide."

Izabella picked up a small mirror from the corner of the desk—one his grandfather must have used—and angled it over the writing. Slowly, with the journal open beside her, the symbols began to make sense.

Along the margin, da Vinci had scrawled mirrored Tuscan Italian, referencing "earth oils," "refined clays," and "the proper tension between lightness and strength." Some passages even included phrases in Latin, especially where he described weightlessness or the natural order.

Izabella's eyes widened. "This isn't metallurgy."

Thomas nodded. "No. It's something else. Some kind of mixture."

He picked up another page, this one looked like a formula broken into stages. A sketch of a hand brushing a clay-like substance onto a surface, followed by a drawing of feathers or small objects floating above it.

"He wasn't trying to smelt a metal," Thomas said. "He was making a material. Something pliable. Something that... bends the rules."

"A paste?" she said. "Or a kind of suspension? Look at this mixing fine dusts and oils in measured ratios."

"And not just any oils," Thomas added. "These are botanical. I think he was extracting them from roots or plants."

She looked around. "Maybe that's what your grandfather was trying to replicate."

Thomas stepped over to a long table and pulled away a canvas cloth. Beneath it was a tray of vials, labeled in his grandfather's handwriting. Some were filled with thick clay, others with golden or silvery liquid suspended in oil.

"I think he got close to the secret mixture," Thomas said. "He might've even finished it."

They both stood in silence, the weight of it sinking in.

Before either could speak again, Izabella turned toward the small ground-level window near the ceiling, narrowing her eyes. "Those men... from the museum... what if they're looking for this?"

Thomas followed her gaze. Maybe they thought the papers had been lost. Maybe they thought no one had figured it out. But they were wrong.

Unknown to Thomas and Izabella, the two men were responsible for orchestrating the Leonardo da Vinci exhibit's arrival in Mobile. They intended to draw out anyone connected to the hidden papers.

Thomas looked back down at the mixture and the glowing pages.

"They're not going to take this from us," he said.

Thomas and Izabella attempt to decipher the lost writings in the artifact room.

Chapter 4

Secrets in the Mirror

All the following week, Thomas couldn't stop thinking about the artifact room.

Now that his time off was over and he was back at work, the hours moved slower than ever. As soon as he clocked out, he rushed to his grandfather's house, now his house, and straight to the artifact room. He unlocked the door and closed it quietly behind him.

The air inside was cool. Dust hung in the light beams spilling in from the small ground-level window. It smelled of cedar, paper, and something faintly earthy.

Thomas dropped his backpack beside the desk and immediately opened the trunk. He spread out the pages he and Izabella had been studying the night before. Some were still resting under glass; others were pinned gently beneath brass weights.

Izabella arrived a few minutes later, letting herself in. She wore her hair up this time and carried a folded notebook and a small mirror under her arm.

"Still haven't slept, have you?" she asked.

"Didn't want to," Thomas said with a grin.

She stepped beside him and unrolled a few more sheets from the pile. One of them had lines of text written in tight, backward scrawl.

"I've been practicing," she said, setting the mirror flat on the desk. "Leonardo wrote most of his personal notes in this mirrored Tuscan Italian—sometimes with a little Latin mixed in."

She angled the mirror and studied the reflection.

"I can make out some of it," she said. "But your grandfather's journal helps a lot."

Thomas nodded, flipping open the worn leather journal. "He was obsessed with the translations. I think he cracked most of it himself. He left margin notes showing the Latin root meanings, sometimes even phonetic clues."

Together, they worked slowly. Izabella traced her finger across the reversed letters while Thomas matched them to the translations. They read phrases like "liquid suspended in stillness" and "applied with control, drawn from earth."

"It's not metallurgy," Izabella said. "It's more like alchemy. But grounded in real processes."

Thomas looked through more sketches. Some showed bowls, mortars, and scales. Others diagrammed the blending of clays, oils, and mineral powders with cryptic ratios and detailed measurements. The symbols for gold and silver kept appearing, alongside strange instructions about timing and temperature. Bronze was also mentioned as an important ingredient.

"This is a formula," Thomas said. "But for what?"

"I don't think he ever says directly," she replied. "Just... hints. And metaphors."

They turned to a section of the journal where Thomas's grandfather had begun reproducing some of the mixtures. Vials sat beside the notebook—each labeled with notes about color, viscosity, and stability. One mixture was a pale golden hue, another thick like clay, and one shimmered faintly under the lamplight.

"Do you think this is the final version?" Izabella asked.

"I'm not sure," Thomas said. "But it looks close. The proportions line up."

He carefully poured a few drops of one vial into a shallow dish and stirred with a glass rod. The mixture moved slowly, but didn't settle the way oil would. It had a strange resistance, almost as if it held itself together.

"It's like nothing I've ever worked with," Thomas said. "And I've tested dozens of materials."

Izabella leaned in. "Whatever this is... I don't think he meant it to be just a pigment."

They exchanged a look—curious, cautious, and quietly amazed.

The room was silent, filled only with the soft creak of wood and the hum of a low desk lamp. Neither of them knew what the mixture could do. Not yet.

But they knew it was extraordinary.

They are beginning to unlock the secret formula.

Then, his eyes scanned the shelves, the scrolls, and the papers spread across the table. He nodded slowly, visibly moved.

"This room still has his presence," he said.

Thomas introduced Izabella, and the three of them stood together for a moment amid the silence of the room.

"I came to see if he left anything behind," Mr. Wilmore said, his voice quiet. "We were close. When he passed, I wondered if the papers had ever surfaced."

Thomas hesitated. "We found some of them. We've been trying to translate and understand them."

Mr. Wilmore's eyes sparkled. "He would've wanted that."

He walked over to a page resting under glass. "Do you know what this is?"

Izabella and Thomas exchanged a glance.

"It's part of a formula," Thomas said.

"More than that," Mr. Wilmore replied. "Your grandfather believed it was da Vinci's attempt to create the perfect pigment. Something to rival nature itself."

"And you believe it?" Izabella asked.

"I didn't. Not at first. But after everything we uncovered... I'm not so sure anymore."

Mr. Wilmore paused, then looked directly at Thomas. "But listen to me carefully, son. There are people in this world who would do anything to get their hands on what you have. I don't just mean collectors. I mean people with power and no conscience. Some would kill for da Vinci's writings."

Thomas swallowed. "You think it's that serious?"

"I know it is," Wilmore said. "So, whatever you do... be careful."

He placed his hat back on his head. "I won't stay long. I just wanted to see it.

I'm glad it's in the right hands."

After he left, the room was quiet again.

Thomas sat down, still processing the encounter. Then he opened his grandfather's journal once more and returned to the last section he had been studying. His fingers brushed the edge of a vellum sleeve, revealing a page tucked inside.

The script was tighter than usual, and the ink had faded with time.

Izabella held it under the mirror and tilted it until the writing became legible. Her lips moved silently as she read, translating bits aloud.

"It says something about motion without force… or maybe weight without gravity."

Thomas leaned in. "That's impossible."

"Maybe," she said. "Or maybe not."

They exchanged a glance. Neither of them spoke for a moment.

Later that night, after Izabella had gone, Thomas stayed in the artifact room, studying the page again. His grandfather's journal sat open beside him, filled with notes about mixtures, ratios, and da Vinci's poetic reflections on the properties of earth and light.

The mixture wasn't something Leonardo had invented for flight.

It might have been something he discovered—accidentally—while chasing something else entirely.

Thomas closed the book slowly.

He didn't say it aloud, but he was beginning to believe it.

Leonardo had done more than sketch ideas.

He had stumbled onto something. And maybe—just maybe—Thomas and Izabella were about to rediscover it.

Mr. Wilmore explains what the papers are.

CHAPTER 6

THOMAS'S PAST

Watching the dying embers in the fireplace, Thomas sat alone in his grandfather's den the next evening. Izabella had gone home for the night, and Mr. Wilmore had left earlier after checking in on him. Thomas ensured the steel door to the artifact room was locked every time he left.

The house, filled with memories and relics of the past, now felt strangely quiet. He found himself lost in thought, reflecting on his childhood and the moments that had shaped him.

He was the middle boy in the family, with two brothers, Chris and Mark, and a sister, Lisa, who was an accomplished dancer. Lisa's love for music and movement often brought the family together. On quiet evenings, she and Thomas would put on old records and dance in the living room just for the fun of it, laughing as they tried to keep up with the rhythm. Sometimes, those moments turned into full family dance nights, where everyone joined in, filling the house with music, laughter, and a sense of togetherness that Thomas would never forget.

He thought back to when he was a boy, always fascinated by flight. Thomas and his brothers would spend hours conducting their own experiments, attempting to defy gravity in any way they could. One of their favorite activities was making hydrogen balloons. They had learned that by mixing Red Devil lye with water inside a Coke bottle and dropping in balls of aluminum foil, a reaction would take place that produced hydrogen gas. They would place a balloon over the top of the bottle resting in a bucket of water, watching with excitement as it filled. Then, they would tie the balloons together and release them, sending them soaring high into the sky.

Many times, they would write letters and notes to people: "If found please write to our address." Once a man wrote back and the balloons traveled half the Gulf Coast from Mobile, Alabama to Jacksonville, Florida. He indicated that they landed on his barn.

Another time, they had taken it a step further, building a large flying disc out of lightweight materials and filling it with the hydrogen balloons. The creation had risen into the sky, drifting for miles before it disappeared. It even made the local news, sparking speculation about a UFO sighting. The incident had left

Thomas both thrilled and terrified. After that, they never built another flying saucer, but the memory of it always stayed with him.

Now, as he sat alone, he thought about the wings at the museum—the very wings Leonardo da Vinci had designed centuries ago. What if a person could really fly? He had always dreamed of it as a child, and now, with the da Vinci secrets, it seemed like more than just a fantasy. Perhaps there might be something in those lost writings that could bring da Vinci's wings to life.

The thought stirred something deep inside him. He had taken a couple of weeks off from work to settle his grandfather's affairs, but now he had returned to his job as a designer at Gauld Equipment, a local machine shop specializing in equipment for paper mills. This had been his focus for years. But now, he found himself at a crossroads.

Thomas leaned back in his chair, staring up at the ceiling, lost in the enormity of it all. The things he and Izabella had uncovered in Leonardo's writings, a formula for something more than a pigment in paint. It would be more than he had ever imagined.

Eventually, exhaustion took over, and Thomas drifted off to sleep, his mind still filled with thoughts of flight and the mysteries waiting to be unraveled.

Thomas and his brothers build a homemade flying saucer with hydrogen balloons.

CHAPTER 7

IZABELLA'S ROOTS

Izabella had always called Mobile, Alabama her home. She had spent her childhood exploring its historic streets, its warm coastal breeze carrying with it the salty air of the bay. Like Thomas, she had attended Saint Dominic's Catholic School. Though they had never been particularly close in those years, they had shared many of the same teachers and classmates.

Izabella grew up in a home filled with curiosity and adventure. She was the eldest of three children, with a younger sister and brother who looked up to her for her sharp intellect and fearless determination. Her mother was a homemaker, tending to the house and keeping the family together, while her father was an archaeologist, spending long months away on excavation sites, uncovering relics from ancient civilizations. He had a deep passion for history, and he instilled that same love in Izabella from an early age.

Unlike most girls her age, Izabella didn't spend her summers at the beach or at malls with friends. Instead, she traveled with her father to archaeological digs, where she watched in fascination as ancient bones and artifacts were carefully extracted from the earth. While other children played with dolls, Izabella was learning how to gently dust off centuries-old relics. She absorbed every lesson her father taught her about the past— how to recognize the layers of history beneath the soil, how to piece together stories from broken pottery and forgotten manuscripts.

It was during these early experiences that she developed a deep appreciation for art and history. She admired how civilizations left behind pieces of themselves in sculptures, paintings, and writings. Her father's enthusiasm for discovery shaped her worldview, giving her a profound respect for those who had come before her, and a hunger to understand them.

This love of history and art stayed with her into adulthood. She pursued degrees in Fine Arts and Archaeology, combining both her passion for artistic expression and the study of ancient cultures. She longed to be part of something bigger—to uncover the hidden truths that had been buried by time.

Now, as a guide at the Mobile Museum of Art, she had the opportunity to share that passion with others. It wasn't just a job for her; it was a calling. Every tour she gave, every historical fact she shared, felt like she was keeping history alive, making sure the stories of the past weren't forgotten.

And yet, despite all her years of study, she never imagined that one day she would be part of a real discovery—one that had been buried for centuries, hidden within the lost writings of Leonardo da Vinci.

Izabella pieces together stories from old pottery.

CHAPTER 8

THE SPARK BETWEEN

Izabella," Thomas said, glancing at the clock. "Are you hungry?"

She looked up from the parchment, eyes slightly unfocused from hours of deciphering. "Starving, actually."

"Good. There's a little Italian place just down the street. It's nothing fancy, but they serve real food—and they don't mind ink-stained hands."

She smiled and untied the scarf she'd wrapped over her hair. "Lead the way."

Thomas locked the steel door to the artifact room.

The restaurant was tucked into a quiet corner of downtown, its brick walls lined with family photos and old wine bottles covered in wax. They sat near the back, away from the soft murmur of other tables. A flickering candle sat between them, and for once, neither of them had a mirror, a scroll, or a flask in hand.

"This is nice," she said, exhaling deeply as the waiter walked away with their order.

"Yeah," Thomas said. "It's good to take a break from the mystery room."

There was a pause—comfortable, not awkward.

Izabella tilted her head. "You know, you haven't changed much since eighth grade."

Thomas blinked. "Really?"

"You still lean your head a little when you're thinking, and you still talk with your hands."

He laughed. "Well, you still squint when you read something fascinating. It's how I knew to pay attention back in class—your face always gave it away."

Izabella grinned. "I remember that day you gave your report on Leonardo da Vinci. You stood up there like you were revealing the secrets of the universe."

"I kind of thought I was," Thomas said, chuckling. "Most of the class thought I was nuts."

"I didn't," she said softly.

Their eyes met for a moment, longer than either expected. Something flickered there—familiar, maybe even inevitable—but unspoken.

Then Izabella's gaze drifted toward the window. Two men from the museum were standing across the street, one writing in a small notebook while the other casually watched the restaurant.

Thomas followed her eyes. "You think they're still following you?"

"They've shown up more than once," she said. "But they're careful. Never close enough to approach—just enough to be seen."

Thomas watched the two men as they turned and strolled down the block.

"They're looking for something they don't understand. And they know we're closer than they are," Isabella said, her tone clam.

Thomas nodded. "Still, we should be careful."

"We will be."

The waiter brought their food, and the conversation shifted to DaVinci topics—the strange taste of one of the clay samples, the bizarre da Vinci diagram they couldn't make sense of, the way her translations sometimes felt like decoding poetry rather than science.

As they stepped back out into the cool evening air, the two men across the street were gone.

They walked in silence for a few blocks before reaching the house.

Thomas paused before opening the door. "You know," he said, "this thing we're chasing—it's bigger than us."

Izabella looked up at him, eyes clear and steady. "That's why we have to see it through."

He opened the door, and the familiar scent of old paper and cedar greeted them.

"Well," she said, brushing hair from her face, "we better get back to it."

There seems to be a spark between Thomas and Izabella as they uncover hidden secrets.

CHAPTER 9
REVELATION

After work on Monday, Thomas and Izabella once again returned to the artifact room. It was becoming more than just a place of study—it was now their makeshift laboratory. The long wooden table was crowded with flasks, weights, ancient scales, and tools from another era. Scrolls, notebooks, and copies of Leonardo da Vinci's mirrored notes were scattered across every surface. Shelves nearby held jars of oils, clays, powdered minerals, and flecks of gold and silver— the raw materials they had painstakingly collected based on Leonardo's writings.

The room was dimly lit by an old desk lamp that cast a warm glow over their experiments. The air smelled of metal, dust, and something faintly floral—an earthy mix from one of the oils Izabella had extracted from a resin tree. They had deciphered most of the formula over the past week, slowly matching da Vinci's poetic descriptions with real-world elements. Some phrases had required Izabella to angle the mirror just right to decode. Others were buried in layers of Tuscan Italian and Latin metaphors.

But now they were ready.

Thomas carefully stirred the mixture in a glass bowl, heating it gently over a small flame. The paste-like substance shimmered slightly, thick and iridescent. It looked like no pigment he had ever seen.

"This is it," he said, breathless.

Izabella nodded, her eyes wide with anticipation. She picked up a small metal coin they had chosen as a test object. Thomas dipped a brush into the shimmering mixture and coated the coin with a thin, even layer.

They waited.

At first, nothing happened. The coin rested on the wooden table, glinting under the lamplight. But then—it shifted. Slowly, gently, it began to lift from the surface.

Izabella gasped. Thomas stepped back in disbelief as the coin hovered several inches above the table, bobbing slightly as if suspended by an invisible thread.

"It worked," he whispered. "It actually worked."

Izabella's hand trembled slightly as she reached toward the coin. "This... this wasn't supposed to happen. He was trying to make a better pigment."

Thomas's eyes were still locked on the coin. "Maybe he did. Maybe he found something by accident."

Izabella turned toward one of the open journals. "It says here to capture the lightness of the heavens in paint'—I thought he meant color."

Thomas smiled, his mind racing. "He meant weightlessness." They looked at each other, both fully aware that this was no longer just about art or history. What they had discovered could change everything.

Izabella whispered, almost afraid to say it aloud. "We just recreated a forgotten discovery. An accident of genius."

Thomas nodded. "And we have the formula. Written down. In da Vinci's own hand."

The coin continued to float in space between them, a quiet symbol of everything that was about to come.

Then Thomas added, his voice low, "Maybe those men at the museum knew more than we thought. Maybe they weren't just after the history... maybe they knew about the anti-gravity potential. Maybe they were after this—Leonardo's secret formula."

The new formula worked!

CHAPTER 10

SHADOWS IN THE CITY

Thomas and Izabella had been spending most of their time at Thomas's grandfather's house, carefully working through the lost writings of Leonardo da Vinci. The house, now legally his, had become more than just a home—it was their sanctuary, their laboratory, and their place of discovery.

But outside their haven, danger lurked. The two mysterious men who had appeared at the museum were still around. They had been spotted walking the streets of Mobile, sometimes near the museum, other times loitering in the city square. It was clear they were still searching for something.

One afternoon, as Izabella finished her shift at the Mobile Museum of Art, she stepped outside and caught sight of them again. They weren't just wandering this time—they were watching her.

A shiver ran down her spine. She hurried down the steps, keeping her pace steady, not wanting to alert them that she had noticed their presence. Her heart pounded in her chest. She needed to tell Thomas.

Meanwhile, back at the house, Thomas was deep in thought when a knock at the door startled him. He opened it to find Mr. Wilmore, his grandfather's old friend, standing on the porch.

"Thomas," he whispered, stepping inside. "I've just seen those two men again – sitting in a car down the street. I don't like it."

Thomas tensed. "You think they know about the papers?"

"I'd bet on it," Mr. Wilmore said. "They may not know that you have them, but they're after something. And I have a bad feeling that they're starting to suspect Izabella knows more than she's letting on."

As if on cue, Izabella arrived, slightly out of breath. "I just saw them again," she said, closing the door behind her. "They were watching me."

Thomas exchanged a worried glance with Mr. Wilmore. "We need to secure the papers better," he said. "If they come looking for them, they need to find something else."

Izabella nodded. "What if we create a fake version of the secret formula? Something convincing enough to throw them off if they ever get their hands on it."

"That might work," Mr. Wilmore said. "Just enough to keep them busy and lead them in the wrong direction."

Thomas opened his notebook. "We can add a few misleading sketches and some altered ingredient ratios. If they try to recreate it, it won't work."

That evening, the three of them worked with quiet urgency. Izabella aged the paper using tea and heat, while Thomas copied the script in mirrored Italian and Latin. Mr. Wilmore added authentic-looking flourishes to make it seem like part of da Vinci's collection.

By midnight, the false code and supporting documents were sealed in an envelope and put on a shelf on the 1st level above the artifact room, easy for them to find.

The real formula, meanwhile, was stored in a waterproof case and buried under the house, secured in an iron box that had once belonged to Thomas's grandfather.

As they finished, Thomas dusted off his hands. "If they come looking, they'll find the fake first."

Mr. Wilmore crossed his arms. "Let's just hope that's enough to buy us some time."

But even as they took precautions, an unsettling feeling lingered in the air. The men wouldn't give up so easily. And none of them knew how far their pursuers were willing to go.

The two men still hanging around, the team works on a convincing fake document.

CHAPTER 11

MR. WILMORE

Mr. Wilmore had spent most of his life in law enforcement, building a reputation as a trusted and fearless offi-cer. Born and raised in Mobile, Alabama, he knew its streets, neighborhoods, and surrounding areas like the back of his hand. His deep familiarity with the city made him an invaluable asset on count-less cases, from high-profile investiga-tions to quiet operations that demanded discretion and care.

Over the decades, Mr. Wilmore served as a detective, working on a wide range of complex cases that required sharp thinking and steady leadership. His calm demeanor and unwavering sense of justice earned him deep respect not only among his peers, but across the entire community. Even after retirement, Wilmore remained a trusted source of wisdom. Law enforcement often consulted him on cases of all kinds, and his reputation for level-headed strategy and precise action made him a natural leader whenever danger arose.

Beyond his work, Mr. Wilmore was known for his quiet strength of character. He was a deeply religious man, attending church regularly and holding fast to a steady belief in God that guided his actions and decisions throughout life. His faith was part of what shaped his loyalty, integrity, and compassion — qualities that made him a protector of those in need.

Mr. Wilmore shared a passion for adventure with Thomas's grandfather. The two had been close friends, living just two doors down from one another. Together, they embarked on countless expeditions — exploring forgotten places, chasing lost legends, and ultimately uncovering the hidden writings of Leonardo da Vinci that would change Thomas's destiny forever.

After the death of Thomas's grandfather, Mr. Wilmore felt a deep sense of responsibility. He knew that the grandfather had left the house to Thomas, and he made it a point to check in on the young man— especially as he sensed Thomas stepping into mysteries far larger than himself. When Mr. Wilmore learned that Thomas had discovered the lost writings of Leonardo, his visits became more frequent, offering quiet support, wisdom, and protection as the danger around Thomas and Izabella grew.

Though his badge had long been retired, Mr. Wilmore's courage and loyalty remained as strong as ever. He was a man trusted to help in moments of peril — a protector who would stop at nothing to safeguard those he cared about, and the extraordinary secret they had uncovered.

Detective Wilmore leading the way on one of his previous cases.

Chapter 12

The Break-In

Thomas sat alone in his grandfather's house, the quiet ticking of an old clock marking time in the stillness. The artifact room, once a place of discovery and wonder, now felt heavy with tension. Izabella had gone home for the evening, and Mr. Wilmore had left earlier after another long discussion about the importance of keeping Leonardo da Vinci's lost writings—and the secret formula—safe.

He leaned back in his chair, eyes tracing the shelves lined with vials, journals, and the mirror they'd used so often. His mind was a whirlwind of everything that had happened: the astonishing discovery of the weightless formula, the forged copy they had created to throw off the men who were watching them, and the constant shadow that followed them through the city.

A faint sound broke his concentration.

It was subtle at first—barely more than a creak. But then came the unmistakable thud of a door being forced open.

Thomas shot up from his chair, heart pounding. He stepped quietly to the edge of the artifact room, pressing himself into the shadows as heavy footsteps echoed above. A crash followed—wood splintering, drawers being yanked open, paper rustling.

They were inside.

He stayed still; every muscle tensed. The intruders moved with purpose. They weren't searching aimlessly, they knew what they were after.

They weren't coming through the heavy steel door of the Artifact room Thomas thought. It was locked and secure. He was safe for now.

Then silence.

Their footsteps retreated, and the house was still again.

Thomas waited a long minute before creeping up the stairs. The front door stood ajar, a cold breeze drifting through. The living room had been ransacked, books and papers strewn across the floor, cushions overturned, drawers pulled out.

The false documents, the fake formula, were gone.

He stood there, staring at the empty space on the shelf where they had been. His fists clenched.

A pounding knock sounded at the door.

Thomas jumped and turned quickly. It was Mr. Wilmore.

"I saw two men jogging away from here," he said breathlessly as Thomas let him in. "I had to check on you."

Thomas let out a breath and motioned for him to follow. "We have a problem."

Mr. Wilmore's eyes scanned the wreckage in the front room, then the artifact room. "They broke in."

Thomas nodded grimly. "They took the fake papers."

A slow, knowing smile crossed Mr. Wilmore's face. "Then they think they have the real ones."

"Exactly," Thomas said. "They'll believe they've won. They might back off for a while if they think the job is done."

But Thomas's jaw tightened. The thought of Izabella being in danger made his stomach twist.

Mr. Wilmore noticed. "You'd better keep an eye on her," he said. "These men might do anything."

Thomas didn't respond right away. He just looked at the empty shelf.

"They'll be watching," Mr. Wilmore added. "Even now, they might be planning their next move."

"Let them," Thomas said. "They're chasing a lie."

But deep down, both men knew—

The worst was yet to come.

The intruders break into Thomas's grandfather's house and take the fake papers as planned.

CHAPTER 13

THE KIDNAPPING

The night air was cool as Izabella locked the museum doors behind her. Because today was its final showing, the Leonardo da Vinci exhibit had brought in more visitors than usual. She was exhausted. She adjusted her bag on her shoulder and started toward her car, the parking lot nearly empty.

That's when she heard footsteps.

Before she could react, a strong arm wrapped around her waist, pulling her back. A hand clamped over her mouth as she struggled, her muffled screams going unheard in the empty lot. The two men—the same ones who had been lurking around for weeks—dragged her toward a black SUV parked at the curb.

The door opened. She kicked and thrashed, but they shoved her inside. The last thing she saw before the door slammed shut was the museum's front sign illuminated in the distance.

Then the vehicle sped off into the night.

Thomas sat at his grandfather's desk, flipping through the da Vinci writings once more, trying to make sense of the deeper implications of the mysterious formula. He was so absorbed in his thoughts that when his phone rang on the desk, it startled him.

He answered it, hands shaking.

"Thomas Patrick," a deep voice said. "If you ever want to see Izabella again, you'll bring us the real lost writings of Leonardo da Vinci."

Thomas's breath caught. He sat up straight. "Who is this? What have you done with her?"

"She's safe—for now. But if you want her to stay that way, you'll do exactly as we say. We know you have the papers, and we know you've been working on them. You'll bring them to us."

"Where?" Thomas demanded.

The man chuckled. "We'll send you the location at midnight. Be ready."

The line went dead.

Thomas stared at the phone in disbelief. A slow, burning anger spread through his chest.

A sudden knock at the front door made him jolt. He crossed the room quickly and opened it to find Mr. Wilmore standing there, his face lined with concern.

"I saw those two men hanging around the museum again tonight," Wilmore said, stepping inside. "I don't like it. Something's wrong."

Thomas's jaw clenched. "They took her."

Wilmore's eyes widened. "What?"

"They kidnapped Izabella," Thomas said, gripping the phone so hard his knuckles turned white. "They just called me. They want the real da Vinci papers—and the formula we deciphered for the anti-gravity material. They know about it."

Wilmore exhaled sharply. "Then we don't have a choice. We need to act fast."

Thomas and Wilmore went straight to work. The first set of fake papers they had created hadn't fooled the men for long. This time, they needed something more convincing—something that looked identical to the originals, with just enough small inaccuracies to mislead anyone trying to recreate the formula. Thomas changed the formula to something he could remember, 8% less metal and 12 % more liquids by weight.

They spent several hours refining the pages, copying Leonardo's mirrored handwriting as closely as possible. Wilmore, with his experience in antique documents, applied aging techniques to make the pages look centuries old. They even used homemade inks derived from iron gall and charcoal to match da Vinci's time.

Finally Thomas said, "They look pretty convincing. They would fool me."

With their work done, Thomas slipped the finished pages into an old satchel and took a deep breath.

"This has to work," he muttered.

Wilmore nodded. "It will."

Moments later, Thomas's phone rang again. A meeting location was given.

"It's a yacht," Thomas murmured. "Less

than a mile off the coast of Dauphin Island."

Wilmore clenched his fists. "I know some important people in the government. You could even say I am one myself. I need to make some phone calls."

Thomas hesitated. "We can't let them know about the papers. But they do need to know Izabella was taken."

Wilmore grabbed the phone. "I'll handle it. You focus on getting to that yacht."

An hour later, Thomas stood at the docks of Dauphin Island, the salty breeze whipping through his hair. The satchel with the fake da Vinci writings was strapped across his shoulder. A small motorboat was waiting for him, arranged by the kidnappers.

The boat's driver, a burly man in dark clothing, eyed Thomas but said nothing. Without a word, Thomas climbed aboard. The engine rumbled to life, and they took off across the dark waters toward the distant glow of the yacht anchored offshore.

As they approached, Thomas saw the massive vessel looming ahead, its deck lined with lights. His stomach twisted.

Izabella was there.

And he was walking straight into their hands.

The world of discovery, danger, and the impossible was still unfolding.

The two men kidnap Izabella to get to the real lost papers. Thomas agrees to meet them on the yacht.

CHAPTER 14

THE WINGS IN THE SHADOWS

Thomas sat on the boat as it cut through the waves, heading toward the yacht where Izabella was being held. The weight of the satchel resting on his lap was nothing compared to the weight pressing against his chest. Inside were the carefully crafted fake writings of Leonardo da Vinci—meticulously designed by Mr. Wilmore to appear authentic.

He glanced back at the shoreline of Dauphin Island, now fading into the distance. The authorities, including Mr. Wilmore, were monitoring everything from afar. They had a plan in place, but Thomas knew the real danger lay ahead. He was about to walk into the hands of the men who had kidnapped Izabella, and there was no guarantee he'd walk out again.

The captain of the small transport boat, a rugged-looking man who had been paid off by Bateau's people, barely acknowledged Thomas as they neared the massive yacht. The vessel loomed on the horizon, a floating fortress gleaming under the morning sunrise.

"You sure you want to do this?" the captain asked gruffly, giving Thomas a sidelong glance. "Once you step on that yacht, there's no turning back."

Thomas inhaled sharply, gripping the satchel's strap tighter. "I don't have a choice."

The boat slowed as it approached the side of the yacht, where a metal ladder had been lowered. A guard stood at the top, looking down at Thomas with an expression of mild amusement. "Welcome aboard," he said, gesturing for Thomas to climb up.

Thomas steeled himself and ascended the ladder. As soon as his feet hit the deck, two more guards appeared, their eyes scanning him warily before nodding in approval. He recognized them as the men that had been at the museum and then outside the restaurant. One of them snatched the satchel from his grasp.

"You'll take me to Izabella first," Thomas demanded, his voice firm despite the fear in his gut.

The guards exchanged smirks, but one of them motioned for Thomas to follow. "Mr. Bateau is waiting for you," the guard said.

They led him inside the lavish interior of the yacht. The corridors were adorned with priceless artifacts, many of which appeared to be stolen relics of historical significance. One room they passed made Thomas freeze—a grand chamber where Leonardo da Vinci's mechanical wings now hung, suspended from the ceiling. The same wings that had once been on display at the museum.

He clenched his jaw and kept walking.

In a dimly lit lounge, seated in a luxurious chair and sipping from a glass of wine, was Henry Bateau—the man behind Izabella's abduction. He was older than Thomas expected, with sharp, calculating eyes and a demeanor of absolute control.

"Ah, Mr. Patrick," Bateau greeted, his voice smooth yet laced with menace. "I appreciate your punctuality."

Thomas barely contained his anger. "Where is she?"

Bateau chuckled, setting down his glass.

"You'll see her soon enough. But first, let's discuss the documents you've brought me."

One of the guards placed the satchel on a nearby table and unzipped it, revealing the aged-looking papers inside. Bateau leaned forward; his eyes gleaming with interest as he carefully picked up one of the sheets. He examined the writing, nodding slowly.

"This is truly fascinating," he murmured. "Leonardo's lost writings... containing the very secrets I have spent years searching for." He turned his gaze back to Thomas. "Tell me, Mr. Patrick, do you understand what you've brought me?"

Thomas kept his expression neutral. "I know it was valuable enough for you to kidnap Izabella over it."

Bateau laughed. "More than valuable. This knowledge is revolutionary. And I'm sure you've figured it out by now—those wings you saw on display?" He smirked. "They were mine. That entire museum exhibit, Mr. Patrick, was arranged by me. The relics, the sketches, the wings... all of it. Its all back on my ship now. I staged the entire show to draw out whoever had access to the real writings."

He stood and they walked slowly toward the onboard artifact room on main deck, the wings were now displayed like a crown jewel hanging from the ceiling. "The wings are impressive, of course. Beautiful, even, Bateau admitted. But I'm not interested in theatrical flight," he said, waving a hand dismissively. "What I want... is the secret Leonardo was truly chasing. A machine that powers itself. Something that defies entropy—a self-sustaining system."

Thomas blinked. "You're talking about perpetual motion?"

Bateau sat down at a desk in the artifact room. There were drawings of energy machines on top. Bateau smiled wider. "Exactly. Energy that requires no fuel, no input—only intelligent design. Leonardo hinted at it in more than one manuscript. A wheel that never stops. A force that renews itself. Imagine what that could do for industry, for power grids... for governments."

He leaned in closer, lowering his voice. "Imagine who would pay to own that kind of technology... or who would go to war to keep others from having it."

Thomas remained quiet, but his thoughts drifted elsewhere. While Bateau was consumed with power and influence, Thomas couldn't stop thinking about the wings. The possibility of human flight—true, self-propelled flight, just as Leonardo envisioned—still held his imagination captive. That, to him, was the real miracle. Not money, not control, not energy monopolies, but freedom. Discovery. The beauty of rising above the earth and proving the impossible was real.

Thomas felt the weight of those words settle. "So that's what this is about. You want to make free energy and then sell it to the highest bidder."

"Yes, but the formula... the formula was missing," Bateau said, his tone sharpening. "Until now."

Bateau hasn't even thought of flying, Thomas thought. It might be his ticket home.

Before Thomas could respond, the doors to the room opened, and two guards led Izabella inside. Her wrists were bound, but otherwise, she looked unharmed. Her eyes widened when she saw Thomas, and she exhaled in relief. Her wrists were then freed.

"Thomas..." she exclaimed as she ran to him.

"Are you alright?" he asked quickly.

She nodded. "I am now." She noticed the energy machine drawings on top of Bateau's desk.

Bateau sighed. "I'm a man of my word, Mr. Patrick. You brought me what I asked for, so I am returning Miss Ricci to you. However," His smile darkened. "You're both staying. Since you two are already quite familiar with these writings, I want you to re-create what's written here... and prove that it works."

Thomas felt a chill run down his spine. They were being forced to bring the formula to life.

Thomas locked eyes with Izabella. They needed to find a way out—before it was too late.

Henry Bateau explains his reason to have the secret formula.

CHAPTER 15

THE OBSESSION OF A MIND UNHINGED

Henry Bateau had always been a man driven by ideas. From a young age, he was captivated by the notion of perpetual motion—machines that could run forever without the need for external power. Where others dismissed the concept as impossible, Bateau saw opportunity. He filled notebook after notebook with designs, gears, and mechanisms, each iteration more elaborate than the last. Teachers called it foolish. Scientists told him it defied physics. But to Henry, it was only a matter of time and discovery.

As he grew older, he turned his obsession into a career. Bateau built prototypes in his private workshop—strange contraptions of brass and steel, balanced on magnets and gyroscopes. They never worked, not the way he hoped, but each failure only deepened his conviction. He wasn't deterred. He was inspired.

Eventually, Bateau stumbled across references to Leonardo da Vinci's lesser-known experiments—not just artistic masterpieces and flying machines, but sketches that hinted at unnatural materials, gravity-defying designs, and coded journals that scholars had yet to fully decipher. That was when Henry's path changed forever.

If anyone in history had come close to discovering the secret of perpetual motion, it was da Vinci. Henry became convinced that hidden within the Renaissance genius's lost writings was a formula—something real. Something that could shield gravity, that could suspend mass, and that could finally allow one of his machines to work.

But the writings were lost... until rumors of a discovery surfaced in an unlikely place: Mobile, Alabama. An obscure collection of Leonardo da Vinci artifacts had made its way to the Museum of Art, and Henry made sure it got there. It was his idea to fund and arrange the exhibit, shipping pieces from collectors and vaults around the world. He curated the show under a false name and remained behind the scenes, knowing the relics would draw out anyone with access to the missing pages.

Henry's plan was simple: observe, identify, and seize. Whoever had the lost writings wouldn't be able to resist the exhibit. And when they appeared, he would be waiting.

He was no longer chasing a theory—he was hunting the final piece of the puzzle.

The moment he confirmed the presence of the real documents, he would act. And he did.

Henry Bateau was not a man bound by conscience or law. His obsession with free energy had eroded any moral boundary he might have once had. To him, the ends always justified the means.

And he would go to no known limits to get what he wanted.

Henry Bateau is a man driven by ideas of developing free energy machines.

Chapter 16

The Mixture Awakens

The laboratory aboard the yacht was a state-of-the-art facility, filled with advanced equipment and materials, many of which were clearly gathered over time through illicit means. Thomas and Izabella stood before an array of clays, oils, powdered minerals, and small vials of ground metals—carefully laid out under the watchful eyes of Bateau's men. The air smelled of heated components, smelted earth, and the faint tang of salt from the open ocean.

Bateau leaned against a nearby workstation, watching them with amusement.

"You see, my dear guests, I am an impatient man, and I do expect results," he said with a smirk. "You have the papers, and now you have the means. Show me the material Leonardo da Vinci was hiding from the world."

Thomas exchanged a look with Izabella, who kept her expression neutral. They had no choice but to proceed. The fake documents had bought them time, but Bateau would not hesitate to turn violent if he suspected deception.

"We'll need a little time," Thomas said, pretending to scrutinize the formulas. "The ratios have to be exact. If we rush it, we risk wasting valuable material."

Bateau nodded approvingly. "Good. Then get started."

The guards stepped back, giving them space to work, though still close enough to intervene. Thomas and Izabella began the delicate process of mixing the components—an alchemical blend of gold, silver dust, and bronze, natural oils, rich clays, and ground stones. They moved with practiced precision. Thomas had committed the real formula to memory, and he'd been careful to alter the written version just enough to protect its secrets.

Now, with the guards watching, he quietly reversed the alterations. He restored the 8% metallic content that he had deliberately left out of the fake formula and rebalanced it by decreasing the liquid ratio by 12%. The effect would be subtle to any observer—but crucial to the success of the compound.

They started with a small batch to ensure success. They transferred the blended mixture into a larger metal basin, Bateau wanted Thomas to use it because the anti-gravity material needed to be eventually made in bulk if it was ever going to coat more than just small test objects. The mixture heated quickly, and within minutes, it began to swirl with vibrant hues forming into a paste that shimmered with layers of gold, pewter, and iridescent blue. Izabella worked beside him, adjusting the heat and timing their intervals.

She glanced at him, eyes reflecting the glow. "It's just like in the writings," she whispered.

Bateau stepped closer; his expression now intense. "Fascinating," he murmured. "Now, let's see if it works."

Thomas dipped a coin into the thick mixture, then held it aloft as the paste cooled to room temperature, remaining pliable with a soft, flexible finish. He set it gently onto the table.

For a long moment, nothing happened. Then slowly, the coin began to tremble, lifting gently until it hovered inches above the surface.

A collective gasp filled the room. Even Bateau's eyes widened. "Incredible," he breathed.

Thomas kept his expression composed, but his heart was thundering. It worked. Even here, under pressure and surveillance, the formula had held.

Bateau turned to his men. "Help them make more," he ordered. "I want a full batch of this material. Enough to coat machinery, plates, anything that can carry weight."

Thomas nodded. "We'll need to prepare another round. The process takes time." He already had a large pot.

He glanced at Izabella, whispering as they gathered more supplies. "I'll adjust the ratios again, but we're making a big batch of the real thing now."

She gave the slightest nod. "How much can we make?"

"Enough," he whispered. "And I've got an idea that may get us out of here."

They worked late into the night, producing a thick, shimmering liquid that pooled into a large, heated container. The material stayed warm enough to remain in liquid form, behaving much like paint—smooth, pliable, and able to coat any surface evenly. The guards, now distracted by excitement and speculation, had grown careless.

Bateau watched with a predator's satisfaction. "You two have done well," he said. "Keep going. Soon, the world will know my name."

Thomas forced a smile, but in his mind, plans were already unfolding.

They had given Bateau what he wanted—just enough to keep him satisfied. Bateau in turn gave Thomas what he wanted. A means of escape!

The mixture is made precisely to the original formula and it works. Bateau is happy and wants more.

CHAPTER 17

THE WATCHERS IN THE DARK

Mr. Wilmore watched as the moon hung low over the Gulf, casting a silver shimmer across the black water. Less than a mile offshore, the yacht sat anchored, its lights glowing softly in the dark, like a ghost ship adrift in the distance. Aboard that vessel were Thomas and Izabella—held against their will, working under pressure, and clinging to hope.

He stood on the deck of a patrol boat in a remote inlet of Dauphin Island, peering through a set of high-powered binoculars. The yacht was in perfect view.

He passed the binoculars to one of the officers beside him. "They're still there. Lights haven't moved. But no activity on the deck."

The officer nodded, then jotted something into a small notebook. Around them, several other boats floated quietly in the dark—unmarked, running without lights, and barely making a sound. It was a joint task force operation. Local law enforcement. A few federal agents. The Coast Guard. All waiting.

Waiting for a sign.

Wilmore stepped back from the rail and pulled a radio from his belt. "Team Alpha, hold positions. Keep all visual contact. Any movement, report immediately."

A voice crackled back. "Roger that. Holding position."

He turned to another officer, a tall man with a weathered face and a calm presence. "We can't go in unless we have confirmation of a crime underway—or a distress signal. We can't risk them getting hurt."

The officer nodded. "Yes, sir."

"It was definitely kidnapping," thought Wilmore, "and ransom of secrets was demanded."

He clenched his jaw. He hated waiting. He hated knowing Thomas and Izabella were out there, possibly in danger, and being forced to work under threat. But they were smart. He had to believe they'd find a way to signal—somehow.

Mr. Wilmore stepped inside the small cabin of the patrol boat and examined the live feed from a long-range telescope camera mounted to the bow. The yacht's silhouette was clear. Too clear. Its stillness was eerie.

"They've got them working on something," he muttered to himself. "But what?"

A young tech officer beside him answered quietly. "We're picking up heat readings on the mid-deck. Looks like the lab's active. Could be high-temperature equipment. Some kind of experiment involving heat."

Wilmore narrowed his eyes. "Then they're close."

He moved back outside and looked up at the stars. Somewhere out there, Thomas was holding the key to something Leonardo da Vinci had hidden for centuries. And somewhere inside, Izabella was still standing with him. That gave Wilmore comfort—and motivation.

He turned to the team again. "I want full surveillance all night. I don't care if a light flickers, I want to know about it."

"Yes sir."

"And when the time comes," Wilmore said, narrowing his eyes toward the distant yacht, "we don't hesitate. We move fast. We take back what's ours. And we bring those two home."

The team nodded, the unspoken weight of the mission hanging in the night air.

They were closer than Bateau would ever know.

Mr. Wilmore leads a team of law enforcement to rescue Thomas and Izabella.

Chapter 18
The Flight
of Leonardo

The soft glow of sunrise bled through the horizon, casting faint orange light across the upper decks of the yacht. The sea was calm, gently rocking the massive vessel in a slow rhythm. Below deck, in the hidden laboratory, Thomas and Izabella stood in silence, staring down at the still-warm mixture they had spent the night creating.

It shimmered in the large basin like liquid gold and silver with swirls of bronze. The air in the room carried the scent of oils and earth, like something ancient. It no longer bubbled or steamed. Instead, it sat—calm, viscous, and glowing softly in the dim light.

"It's ready," Thomas whispered.

Izabella nodded, her heart racing.

They had waited hours for it to cool to a temperature that would allow contact with skin. Now, as they stood in their work clothes, both of them were breathing hard, not just from exhaustion, but from anticipation.

Thomas dipped his fingers into the mixture first. It was warm, but not uncomfortably so. Smooth and pliable. Like the finest paint ever created.

With barely a word between them, they got to work.

They coated their hands, their arms, their faces. They rubbed the mixture across their clothes, their shoes, their hair—every inch of themselves needed to be covered. The substance didn't soak in. It adhered lightly to the surface, forming a thin, shimmering layer that held its sheen even as it dried.

At first, they felt nothing unusual. But within minutes, the weight in their legs seemed to lighten. The floor beneath them no longer felt as firm.

Izabella looked at Thomas, her eyes wide. "Do you feel it?"

He took a step and almost floated. "Yeah," he said softly. "I feel it."

They weren't completely weightless. But close. Their steps barely made a sound, and their bodies lifted, as though gravity had loosened its grip.

The lab was silent except for their quiet movements and the creaking of the yacht. Thomas quietly took the fake papers. He knew what he had to do.

Thomas and Isabella slowly worked their way up to the ship's artifact room, where the mechanical wings hung suspended from the ceiling, gently swaying with the motion of the yacht. They were near a set of double doors that led directly to the outer main deck. He stepped beneath them, carefully unhooking the harness from the ceiling rig with Izabella's help. These were da Vinci's wings—his design brought to life.

Bateau had brought them aboard. Of course he had. He wanted everything in one place: the formula, the minds to make it, and now in Thomas's mind the wings to prove it.

They were lighter than they appeared—crafted from a combination of wood, canvas, and metal fittings. The design was simple, elegant, and adjustable. A marvel.

He turned to Izabella. "Help me get these on."

They worked together in silence, tightening the straps across his chest and back. As the final buckle snapped into place, Thomas stood still for a moment, balancing himself.

The material coating his body reacted subtly to the wings' weight. Instead of dragging him down, they seemed to lift with him.

Izabella stepped back, her breath catching. "Thomas..."

He tested a few steps. Then a hop, then several wing flaps. Then he lifted.

His feet hovered a full foot above the floor. He steadied himself with outstretched arms. He was flying.

"I think it's working," he said, grinning.

A noise echoed faintly from the deck above.

The guards would wake up soon.

Thomas looked at Izabella. "We need to go. Right now."

She nodded, and together they opened the double doors and stepped out onto the deck. The rising sun bathed the top deck in gold.

Thomas threw all the fake papers into the dark waters of the Gulf. He didn't want anyone to ever discover them!

Thomas adjusted the wings strapped to his back. Izabella, already coated in the shimmering material they had created in the lab, wrapped her arms around him from behind. They had worked in silence through the night, applying the strange clay-and-metal mixture to their skin, clothes, and hair. It had cooled to a warm, pliable paste—thick and smooth like paint—and once coated, it had started to change them. They weren't floating entirely, but they felt lighter, their bodies buoyant, almost immune to gravity's pull.

Now, standing on the deck with the wings spread wide and dawn rising before them, they waited.

Izabella leaned in. "Are you ready?"

Thomas didn't answer right away. He felt the wind swirl around them, catching the tips of the wings, lifting his heels slightly off the wooden deck.

Then it happened.

The wind lifted them—effortlessly.

No jump. No launch. Just a sudden upward sweep, a glide into the morning sky as if nature itself had given them permission to fly.

This is going to be a flight to remember.

Thomas and Izabella, now covered with the mixture and nearly weightless, take flight using Leonardo's wings.

CHAPTER 19

A FLIGHT TO REMEMBER

The sky was beginning to lighten as the first rays of dawn touched the Gulf horizon. A golden glow spread across the sky, casting soft light over the open waters and the polished deck of the yacht. From a distance, the patrol boats could see movement on the deck—two figures standing one behind the other, framed against the rising sun.

They rose above the yacht, gliding smoothly with the Gulf breeze guiding their path. Izabella tightened her grip around Thomas's chest. Her voice was soft in his ear.

"I still can't believe this is happening."

Thomas chuckled; a light laugh carried by the wind. "Neither can I. But hey... I'm glad I'm flying with you, I've always liked you even in grade school, Izabella."

She grinned, pressing her cheek to his back. "Well, I've always thought you were pretty great too, Thomas."

He smiled. "So, I guess if I said, 'Hey, let's hang out sometime together...'"

She laughed mid-flight. "I guess I can't hang out any better than I'm hanging out now!"

Their laughter echoed in the wind as they soared.

Down below, on one of the patrol boats circling just a mile from the yacht, Mr. Wilmore stood on the deck with binoculars raised. The sun caught the glint of the wings, and he gasped. "That's them," he said. "It's Thomas... and Izabella."

The officers nearby rushed to the railing, watching in disbelief as the two figures soared into the sky.

"That's our signal," Wilmore said. "Move in!"

The patrol boats powered forward, waves breaking beneath them as they closed the distance to the yacht. Within minutes, armed officers boarded the vessel. Bateau's men, caught off guard, surrendered without a fight.

Bateau himself was furious, caught not just by law enforcement, but by the sheer impossibility of what he had just witnessed.

"They flew," he muttered. "They actually flew…"

On the shore, Thomas and Izabella landed softly on the sand of Dauphin Island. They were met by officers and Wilmore, who approached in awe.

"Son," one officer said, "we're going to need to take possession of those wings."

Thomas nodded without hesitation. "That's fine."

"But the real secret is not in the wings," thought Thomas. "It's in da Vinci's formula."

Wilmore stepped forward; his expression serious. "We'll need to find a place for those lost writings, too. If the wrong people get their hands on them—"

"They won't," Thomas said. "We'll hide them again. Somewhere safe."

Izabella gave him a knowing smile, and Thomas smiled back.

"We've done the impossible," he said, turning toward the rising sun.

Thomas and Izabella land safely on Dauphin Island.

Epilogue

With the danger behind them, Thomas, Izabella, and Mr. Wilmore worked together to ensure that Leonardo da Vinci's lost writings — and the incredible formula hidden within — would never again fall into the wrong hands. The artifact room, though secure, no longer seemed enough. Quietly, and with great care, they found a new place, a place far safer and known only to them, where the writings and formula could remain hidden for generations. There, the secrets of flight, of weightlessness, and of da Vinci's genius would rest undisturbed, protected by their promise to guard it always.

Meanwhile, Bateau and his men were brought to justice. Their crimes could not be ignored, and the courts showed no mercy. Found guilty of kidnapping, theft, and conspiracy, they were sentenced to many years in prison, with no hope of parole. The threat they posed was gone forever.

Time moved on. In the year that followed, Thomas and Izabella grew closer still, bound by their shared trials and the wonder of what they had discovered together. At last, with joy and quiet celebration, they married, beginning a new chapter side by side. Together, they explored lost places and sought forgotten truths, always carrying with them the spirit of discovery that had first brought them together — and wouldn't you know it? Little Thomas came along to join them in their adventures, eager to discover new things right alongside his mother and father.

And perhaps, one day, the world might come to know the full story of what Thomas, Izabella, and Mr. Wilmore had protected — secrets hidden from Bateau and his men, kept safe until the time when the world would truly need them.

ABOUT THE AUTHOR

THOMAS PATRICK is a new author with a passion for blending history, science, and imagination into captivating tales. He holds a Bachelor of Science in Mechanical Engineering and has spent his career working in chemical plants, paper mills, and machine shops, where he gained practical experience in drafting and drawing mechanical designs. This work deepened his understanding of how mechanical systems function and how organic chemistry shapes the world around us. He is inspired by his lifelong love of the sciences and physics.

Thomas lives in Mobile, Alabama, with his wife, Pamela Patrick, and together they have four children who have blessed them with grandchildren. He hopes to write another story based on an inspiring idea that continues to fuel his imagination, sharing new adventures and discoveries with his readers.

The Flight of Leonardo is his first novel; a reflection of his fascination with invention, discovery, and the enduring mysteries left behind by great minds like Leonardo da Vinci.

You have a story.
We want to publish it.

Everyone has as a story to tell. It might be about something you know how to do, or what has happened in your life, or it may be a thrilling, or romantic, or intriguing, or heartwarming, or suspenseful story, starring a cast of characters that have been swimming around in your imagination.

And at Wyatt & Sons Publishers, we can get your story onto the pages of a book just like the one you are holding in your hand. With professional interior design and a custom, professionally designed cover built just for you from the start, you can finally see your dream of being an author become reality. Then, you will see your book listed with retailers all over the world as people are able to buy your book from wherever they are and have it delivered to their home or their e-reader.

So what are you waiting for? This is your time.

visit us at

www.wyattpublishing.com

for details on how to get started becoming a
published author right away.